DA

W9-AHH-362

MAKE ROOM
FOR ELISA

By Johanna Hurwitz

The Adventures of Ali Baba Bernstein
Aldo Applesauce
Aldo Ice Cream
Aldo Peanut Butter
Ali Baba Bernstein, Lost and Found
Baseball Fever
Busybody Nora
Class Clown
Class President
The Cold & Hot Winter
DeDe Takes Charge!
"E" Is for Elisa
The Hot & Cold Summer
Hurray for Ali Baba Bernstein
Hurricane Elaine
The Law of Gravity
Much Ado About Aldo
New Neighbors for Nora
New Shoes for Silvia
Nora and Mrs. Mind-Your-Own-Business
Once I Was a Plum Tree
The Rabbi's Girls
Rip-Roaring Russell
Roz and Ozzie
Russell and Elisa
Russell Rides Again
Russell Sprouts
School's Out
Superduper Teddy
Teacher's Pet
Tough-Luck Karen
The Up & Down Spring
Yellow Blue Jay

Johanna Hurwitz

MAKE ROOM FOR ELISA

Illustrated by Lillian Hoban

Morrow Junior Books
New York

NARBERTH
COMMUNITY LIBRARY

Text copyright © 1993 by Johanna Hurwitz.
Illustrations © 1993 by Lillian Hoban.

All rights reserved. No part of this book may be reproduced or utilized
in any form or by any means, electronic or mechanical, including photocopying,
recording, or by any information storage and retrieval system,
without permission in writing from the Publisher.
Inquiries should be addressed to William Morrow and Company, Inc.,
1350 Avenue of the Americas, New York, NY 10019.

Printed in the United States of America.
1 2 3 4 5 6 7 8 9 10
Library of Congress Cataloging-in-Publication Data
Hurwitz, Johanna.
Make room for Elisa / by Johanna Hurwitz ; illustrated by Lillian Hoban.
p. cm.
Summary: The adventures of five-year-old Elisa as she attends her brother's recital,
gets new eyeglasses, moves with her family to a new apartment,
and welcomes the new baby.
ISBN 0-688-12404-6.—ISBN 0-688-12429-1 (lib. bdg.)
[1. Brothers and sisters—Fiction. 2. Family life—Fiction. 3. Apartment houses—
Fiction.] I. Hoban, Lillian, ill. II. Title. PZ7.H9574Mak 1993
[Fic]—dc20 92-45864 CIP AC

In memory of a very special person.
She had room in her heart for everyone:
Marlene Levins.

Contents

MAKE ROOM
FOR ELISA

Russell's Recital

Elisa Michaels was Russell's little sister. She had
just turned five. That made her four years younger
than Russell. Russell could read and Elisa couldn't.
But already Elisa could recognize all the letters of
the alphabet. She knew her numbers, too. Elisa
knew how to tell time if it was one o'clock or two
o'clock or three o'clock. However, she still got con-

fused when it was the times in between the hours.

Russell could ride a two-wheel bike. Elisa's legs didn't even reach the pedals on Russell's big bike. But when she got a little bigger, she was going to learn how to ride. Her father had promised that he would teach her.

There was another thing Russell did that Elisa didn't. He belonged to the Cub Scouts.

"Cub Scouts is just for boys," said Russell smugly.

"I don't care," said Elisa. "I can be a Brownie." Mrs. Michaels had promised Elisa that when she was older she could join. Brownies were only for girls, and Russell could never be a Brownie. Brownies got to wear uniforms with yellow scarves, just like the Cub Scouts. She could hardly wait until she was old enough to join.

Nowadays Russell was learning how to do something new. He was learning how to play the violin. Last September he had begun taking lessons after school every Thursday at the Amsterdam House of Music. He had a special small-sized violin to practice on. It had strings and a bow. Russell held the violin under his chin, just like grown-up violinists did on TV. He moved the bow along the strings to make music. At first he could play only a few easy songs like "Row, Row, Row Your Boat" and "Yankee Doodle." But gradually he learned to play other melodies as well.

Often, while Russell was practicing his lessons, Elisa sang along. She knew the words to most of the songs he played. Once, when Russell wasn't looking, Elisa tried to play the violin too. She couldn't make any music at all, just funny squeaky sounds. And what was worse, her mother had scolded her.

"The violin is not a toy," said Mrs. Michaels. "It could break if you aren't careful. You must keep your hands off of it," her mother insisted.

"I know that," Elisa said, pouting. She had a little xylophone to play, but it wasn't a real instrument. She wanted to make real music like Russell. Elisa thought her brother looked very important carrying his violin case to and from his lessons.

"When you are a little older, you can also take music lessons," Mrs. Michaels promised Elisa. "How would you like to learn how to play the piano?"

No one would know if you took piano lessons, because you couldn't carry the instrument around with you, Elisa thought. But she still liked the idea. Her teacher at the Sunshine Nursery School played the piano, and sometimes Elisa liked to push the keys and try and make music too.

"Yes! Yes!" she shouted. "I want to take piano lessons."

"We don't have a piano," Russell pointed out. "You can't take piano lessons if you don't have a piano."

"Well, perhaps we shall get a piano one of these days," Mrs. Michaels said.

"There's no place to put a piano," said Russell, looking around.

"I hope we will be getting more space before too long," said Mrs. Michaels. "We certainly could use more room, especially now." Elisa didn't know what her mother meant by that. Apartments didn't grow bigger. It seemed unlikely there would ever be enough room for a big instrument like a piano in their home. So maybe she would never be able to learn how to play the piano after all, she thought sadly.

"I hope we're not going to move," said Russell, looking at his mother anxiously. "I like it right here."

Mrs. Michaels shrugged her shoulders and didn't say anything more on the subject.

One month later, in May, the Amsterdam House of Music held its annual recital. All the students would have a chance to perform for their family and friends.

"Will Daddy come to hear me play?" Russell wanted to know.

"Yes. He's going to leave work early so he'll be able to attend."

"I'm going to come too," said Elisa.

"Does she have to come?" Russell complained. "I don't think she's old enough to attend a recital."

"I am so old enough," said Elisa.

"I'm sure Elisa will be a perfect member of the audience," said Mrs. Michaels. "She'll sit quietly and listen to the music, just like everyone else."

"She'll probably start singing," said Russell. "The way she does at home."

"I won't sing at the recital. I promise," said Elisa. "I'll be very good if you let me come."

"Well, okay," said Russell grudgingly. "You can come if you promise not to open your mouth."

"You said that there's going to be punch and cookies after the recital. How can I eat if I don't open my mouth?"

"You can open your mouth to eat *after* the music is over. But don't talk or sing or even whisper during the recital," Russell instructed.

"Okay," Elisa agreed.

She was very pleased that she was going to the recital and that she would hear all the other music students as well as Russell. Their neighbors Nora and Teddy Resnick, who lived upstairs on the seventh floor of their apartment building, would be performing at the recital too. Nora took flute lessons, and Teddy was learning to play the violin, just like Russell.

On the afternoon of the recital, Russell and Elisa got all dressed up. Russell wore a jacket and a necktie. Elisa wore her party dress and real shoes instead of sneakers. Her mother combed her hair and put a ribbon in it too. Elisa looked in the mirror to admire her appearance. She felt something was missing. But what?

Elisa went to the bedroom and searched through her drawers. Finally she found it: the necklace of colored macaroni that she had made in school. Each piece of macaroni had been painted a different color: red, green, blue, yellow, or purple. Then Elisa had strung them together. Elisa thought that the necklace looked very pretty, and she always felt good when she wore it.

"You're not going to wear those old macaronis to my recital," Russell protested when he saw her.

"Yes I am. It's my special necklace, and I can wear it if I want to," said Elisa.

"Mom!" Russell shouted. "Look at Elisa. She looks silly wearing those old macaronis."

"No I don't!" Elisa shouted back. Sometimes Russell made her very angry.

"Yes you do."

"We don't have time to argue about this," said Mrs. Michaels looking at her wristwatch. "Russell, you look very handsome, and if Elisa feels pretty wearing her necklace, she should wear it."

Russell picked up his violin case. "I think it's dumb. Macaroni is to eat. Who ever heard of wearing it around your neck?"

"Don't forget your music," Mrs. Michaels reminded Russell.

She gave him a hug. "I know you're feeling nervous about performing in front of so many people," she told him. "But you've practiced a lot and know it all perfectly. You are going to be just great."

"Yeah. Maybe," Russell mumbled.

He got his music book, and the three of them left the apartment.

They were going to meet Mr. Michaels at the recital.

Mr. Charles, Russell's violin teacher, had several students in addition to Russell and Teddy. His students sat together on folding chairs off to one side of the large room where the recital was being held. Elisa saw Nora and the other performers sitting there too. Nora jumped up from her seat to greet them. "I like your macaroni necklace," she told Elisa.

Russell scowled. "See you later," he said to his mother as he moved toward a seat.

Mrs. Michaels reached out and patted his shoulder. "Good luck," she told him.

Russell's face turned red. "Yeah," he muttered.

8

"We need to save a seat for Daddy," Elisa reminded her mother as they looked for a place for themselves. The seats toward the front of the room were already filled with members of the audience.

Mrs. Michaels found three empty seats at the back of the room. On each seat was a program with the names of the performers and the music they were going to play. Elisa picked up her program before she sat down. Even though she couldn't read yet, she was able to find Russell's name on the program. She knew he was going to play "She'll Be Coming Round the Mountain" when it was his turn. It was one of her favorite songs.

More and more people were filling the seats. Elisa looked around the room. She was glad she was in the audience and not performing. It would be scary to have to stand up in front of so many people and play the violin.

As she waited for the recital to begin, Elisa played with her macaroni necklace, turning it round and round her neck. She could never decide which color macaroni was the prettiest. Was it the red, or the purple, or the —

"May I sit next to you?" a voice asked her.

9

Elisa looked up. It was her father.

"This *is* your seat. We're saving it for you," she told him. "Russell is over there." She pointed to the area where Russell and the other music students were sitting.

Mrs. Michaels reached over to greet her husband.

Just then Mr. Charles went to the front of the room and held his hand up in the air to get everyone's attention.

"Welcome, welcome," he said when everyone had quieted down.

"I'm glad you could all join us this afternoon. We're going to hear some fine music. All of the children have been making excellent progress. I'm very proud of them and I know you are too."

Elisa smiled. She was proud of Russell. Even when he scolded her or complained about things she did, she still liked him. She knew he would be very good at the recital. He had been practicing his piece for a long time now.

First on the program was a group of half a dozen boys and girls with violins. They looked almost as young as Elisa. Together they played "Twinkle, Twinkle, Little Star." Elisa remembered her promise, and even though she knew the words, she kept her mouth closed all through the music. She sat quietly, but her hands kept fingering her macaroni necklace.

When the children finished their piece, everyone applauded. The children played a second one, "Row, Row, Row Your Boat." The applause was even louder when that was over. Then another group of performers came up to the front.

Russell was not performing with anyone else. He was the only boy his age playing alone. When it was his turn, he stood all by himself in front of the room. Elisa thought he looked very grown up in his jacket and necktie. His hair was slicked back the way it was when he came home from the barbershop. He looked very handsome, but he also seemed even more nervous than before.

Everyone waited for Russell to begin. He stood holding his violin, but he didn't start playing.

"Poor Russell!" Mrs. Michaels whispered to her husband.

"It's stage fright," Mr. Michaels whispered back.

"What can we do to help him?" asked Mrs. Michaels helplessly.

Mr. Michaels shrugged his shoulders. He didn't seem to know either.

Elisa had listened to her brother practicing so often that she could hear the music clearly in her head even without Russell playing it now. Suddenly the music burst out of Elisa's mouth. She heard herself singing the words *"She'll be coming round the mountain when she comes. She'll be coming round the mountain when she comes . . ."*

A woman next to Elisa began to sing the words too. Soon everyone around them joined in the singing.

When Elisa realized what had happened, she blushed a bright red. She had promised Russell she wouldn't open her mouth, and she had broken her promise. Even worse, now everyone else in the room had joined in the song. Elisa felt her face getting hotter and hotter. Her fingers twirled the macaroni necklace around her neck. What was Russell going to say about this?

Suddenly the string holding Elisa's necklace together broke in her hand. Dozens of macaroni, painted red, blue, green, yellow, and purple, fell from her neck and landed on her lap before rattling onto the wooden floor. Some of the people around her leaned over and picked up the macaroni as they continued singing.

Elisa's father leaned over and squeezed her hand. "Good girl. You broke the tension," he whispered to her. Elisa didn't know what he meant. She had broken her promise to keep quiet and she had broken her necklace. But when she looked at Russell, she saw that Mr. Charles was standing next to him. They were singing along with everyone else. That surprised her.

When the song ended, Mr. Charles leaned over and whispered something in Russell's ear. Russell smiled and nodded his head.

The audience quieted down as Mr. Charles returned to his seat. Russell put the violin under his chin again and began to play. Elisa could hear that he played the whole melody without a single mistake. When Russell finished playing, everyone clapped very loudly. Mr. and Mrs. Michaels

clapped louder than anyone else.

Other students performed after Russell, including Nora and Teddy. One girl played a piano piece called "Für Elise." Mrs. Michaels leaned over and whispered that it meant "For Elisa." If she ever took piano lessons, Elisa was going to be sure to learn how to play that.

When the recital was over, Elisa worried what Russell would say to her. He'd probably be furious because she sang during the recital. She had broken her necklace, too.

But when they were drinking their punch and eating the cookies that were set out, Russell didn't even mention what Elisa had done. He looked relieved that the recital was over.

Nora came over to Elisa and Russell. "Your necklace is gone," she said to Elisa. "What happened to it?"

"I broke it," said Elisa. "I broke it when I started singing," she admitted.

"You can always paint some more macaroni and make another one."

"Elisa is very good at painting," said Russell.

Elisa smiled proudly. It wasn't every day that Russell gave her a compliment. When Nora walked away, Russell said, "I'm glad you came to my recital."

"Aren't you angry that I sang?" asked Elisa, amazed.

"I was at first," Russell admitted. "But when everyone was singing, it sounded good, and I stopped being nervous."

"You played perfectly," said Elisa. "You didn't make a single mistake."

"I know," said Russell with satisfaction. "I'm sorry I said bad things about your macaroni necklace."

"I know," said Elisa.

"What's for supper tonight?" Russell asked as they were walking home.

"You'll never guess," laughed Mrs. Michaels.

"Spaghetti?" asked Russell.

"Chicken?" asked Elisa.

"Meat loaf?" suggested Mr. Michaels.

"No. You're all wrong," said Mrs. Michaels. "I

prepared it earlier in the day so it would be ready for supper. All I have to do when we get home is heat it up and cut up some salad."

"What is it?" asked Russell.

"Macaroni and cheese."

"E" Is for Eye Chart

At Elisa's friend Jessica's birthday party, everyone got a box of pastel chalks. Elisa thought that was better than candy! She had a small chalkboard at home, so she could draw on it with the pastels. She had never seen such wonderful red and blue and yellow chalks before. Up till now all she had owned was white.

"I know what," said Elisa as she and her mother walked home from the party. "I could draw pictures on the sidewalk, too." Lots of times she had noticed that other people had drawn on the sidewalk or the street with chalk.

"You can draw in the park," suggested Mrs. Michaels.

"I could draw in front of our apartment building too," declared Elisa with delight.

"No. I don't think you should draw in front of our building," said her mother. "It will look too messy."

Elisa was disappointed about that. But she did take her new chalks to the park the next day and made several big pictures there.

Elisa loved drawing and painting. She had poster paints, watercolor paints, markers, and crayons. Hardly a day went by that Elisa didn't draw a few pictures. The best ones were hung on the refrigerator or on the walls in the bedroom she shared with Russell. Others her mother mailed to Elisa's grandparents.

One rainy day when Elisa was sitting and painting a picture of herself playing in the park, her mother noticed something.

"Elisa, why do you lean so close to the paper?" she asked. "You're going to paint your nose if you aren't careful."

"Paint my nose!" Elisa laughed at the thought of it. "I won't paint my nose," she said.

But after that, Mrs. Michaels watched her daughter, and she noticed that Elisa held books close to her eyes when she looked at them. Sometimes Elisa seemed to be squinting, too.

"I think I had better take Elisa to get her eyes checked. She may be nearsighted," said Mrs. Michaels to her husband.

"What's nearsighted?" asked Elisa.

"It means you can only see things that are near you and can't see things that are farther away so well."

"I can't see things at school," said Elisa, nodding her head in agreement.

"You can't? Oh dear, I wish I had realized that earlier," said her mother, sighing.

"I can see them when I am at school, but they're too far away to see now," Elisa explained. "I don't know if Nibbles the guinea pig is sleeping or eating right now."

Mr. Michaels laughed. "Of course not," he said. "But can you see what he's doing when you are in the classroom?"

"Of course," said Elisa.

"Well, nevertheless, I'm going to take Elisa to an eye doctor," said Mrs. Michaels. So she made an appointment, and a few days later Elisa and her mother, accompanied by Airmail, Elisa's favorite doll, went to get Elisa's eyes examined.

Before they left home, Mrs. Michaels had quizzed Elisa on the letters of the alphabet. "The doctor will show you a chart with lots of letters. Some are big and some are small. He'll want you to tell him which ones you can see," her mother said. "So I want to be sure you know how to recognize all the letters. If you see a letter but don't remember what it is called, the doctor may not realize that you can actually see it."

"How do they check little kids who don't know their ABC's?" asked Russell.

"I think they just use the letter E," said Mrs. Michaels. "But sometimes the letter is on its side or upside down. Then you can point which way you see the letter facing."

COMMUNITY LIBRARY

"The letter E!" said Elisa. "That's my favorite letter. Will I see that?" she asked.

"We'll soon find out," said Mrs. Michaels.

They had a short wait in Dr. Adler's office until it was their turn. Elisa's mother had promised that it wouldn't hurt to have her eyes checked by the doctor, but Elisa was still glad to have Airmail with her for comfort. She held tightly to her doll when they went into the examination room.

After all her review of the ABC's, Elisa and her mother were surprised to see that Dr. Adler's eye chart didn't have any letters at all. It was made up of numbers. Luckily Elisa knew all her numbers without any problem. She read off all the numbers that she could see. But some were too teeny-tiny for her eyes. Then Dr. Adler had Elisa look into a machine. There were no numbers or letters to see, just a bright blue light. He also put drops into her eyes. Elisa clutched Airmail tightly, but it didn't hurt at all. It was like getting water in her eyes when she took a bath.

In the end Dr. Adler turned to Elisa. "I have some big news for you," he said.

"What?" asked Elisa, squeezing Airmail.

"You're going to get eyeglasses."

"Me?" asked Elisa. She could hardly believe it. Eyeglasses were for big people. Eugene Spencer, a big boy who lived in her apartment building, wore glasses. Mrs. Wurmbrand, another neighbor who was very, very old, wore glasses. Miss Rose, her nursery-school teacher, wore glasses. Even her parents and Russell didn't have eyeglasses. It would be a big surprise for Russell when she came home wearing glasses, Elisa thought.

It turned out that Elisa wouldn't get her eyeglasses right away. First she had to go with her mother to a special store that sold glasses. There she tried on many frames that didn't have any glass inside them at all. Elisa looked at herself in a mirror. Did she want round frames or oval ones? Did she want brown frames or blue ones? Elisa thought she did not look like herself with the frames on. She looked like she was wearing a Halloween costume.

At home Elisa made her own chart with numbers and tested Airmail's eyes. Airmail did not need glasses. Elisa tested her other dolls too. None of them needed glasses.

24

"I will be the only one in this family with glasses," said Elisa proudly.

"Big deal," said Russell.

But he did ask to try on Elisa's glasses when she got them two days later.

"Will you know it's me if I am wearing my glasses?" she asked her grandmother over the telephone.

"Absolutely. Positively. You won't be able to fool me. I'll always know it's you," said her grandmother.

"Good," said Elisa.

She was feeling pretty good about the eyeglasses. She had decided on round red ones, and she felt very grown up when she wore them. Best of all, maybe even better than having something that Russell didn't, was the way things looked. Her paints seemed so much brighter now that she was wearing glasses. The red was redder and the blue was bluer. Everything looked special, just like she did.

"Is this my Elisa?" asked Mrs. Wurmbrand when she saw Elisa wearing her glasses for the first time.

"Yes it is," said Elisa.

"Those glasses make you look so grown up," said their neighbor.

"I am," said Elisa. "Soon I'm going to be in kindergarten. I'll go to the same school where Russell goes, too."

"My goodness," said Mrs. Wurmbrand, smiling at Elisa. "Just yesterday you were a little baby."

Sometimes grown-ups said such silly things, Elisa thought. Yesterday she had gotten her new glasses. She wasn't a baby then at all. Mrs. Wurmbrand must have forgotten.

Big News

One Saturday morning in late May, Russell got very angry at Elisa. He was in a hurry to go to a Cub Scouts meeting and was all dressed in his blue uniform. But the yellow scarf that tied under his shirt collar was missing.

"I know I left it on the top of the chest of drawers," he complained to his mother.

"It can't have gone far. It doesn't have legs," said Mrs. Michaels. She was sitting on a kitchen chair and resting as she looked at the mail. She had just brought it upstairs from the mailbox in the building's lobby.

Elisa was sitting at the kitchen table, finishing her breakfast. She didn't pay any attention to Russell. She was too busy picking out all the red cereal bits in her bowl. Next she would eat the green ones.

"Well you come and look," demanded Russell. "I can't go to my meeting without it."

"Calm down," Mrs. Michaels said to Russell. "I'm resting my legs for a few minutes. Look in your drawer. That's where it should be. It doesn't belong on top of the chest."

"How come you're always resting these days?" Russell asked. He ran back to the room he shared with Elisa. "Look at this!" he shouted when he returned to the kitchen a couple of minutes later. He was holding Airmail, Elisa's rag doll, by the hair. Around Airmail's neck was the missing scarf.

Elisa looked up from her bowl of cereal. She had

forgotten that Airmail had borrowed the scarf to play dress-up.

Russell yanked the scarf off of the doll and threw the doll on the floor. "Elisa has no right to take my things!" he shouted. "I don't have any privacy around here. I don't play with her dolls. And I don't want her touching any of my things."

Elisa bent down and picked up her doll. "Airmail only borrowed it for a little while," she protested. She kissed her doll and said, "She didn't tear it or get it dirty or anything."

"I don't care!" shouted Russell. "Don't you dare touch any of my stuff again. Do you hear me?"

Tears welled in Elisa's eyes behind her new glasses. "Cub Scouts are supposed to share," she told her brother.

"Says who?" Russell demanded.

"Okay, let's take it easy here," said Mrs. Michaels. "Russell, you'd better put your scarf on and get going if you don't want to be late for your meeting. And Elisa, here is a job for you. A letter for Mr. and Mrs. Mitchell got into our mail by mistake."

The Mitchells were neighbors who lived on the fourth floor. From time to time the letter carrier accidentally mixed up the Mitchells' and the Michaelses' mail because their names were similar.

"Will you please take it to them?" Mrs. Michaels asked her daughter.

Elisa sniffed back her tears. She nodded her head and smiled. Russell was always the one who went upstairs on errands. This would be the first time she went upstairs all alone.

"It's apartment four-H," her mother reminded her. "Do you know which one that is?"

"Yes, yes," said Elisa, jumping up and down.

"Good," said Mrs. Michaels, handing Elisa the letter for their neighbors.

Elisa walked up the two flights of stairs from the second floor, where her apartment was. She looked at the numbers and letters on all the doors and located 4H. Then she rang the doorbell.

Mrs. Mitchell opened the door. "Why, goodness me. It's little Marissa," she said.

"I'm not Marissa. I'm Elisa," said Elisa.

"Of course, of course. I get confused sometimes. What can I do for you, honey?"

"Nothing," said Elisa. "But I brought you some mail that got in our box by mistake." She handed the envelope to her neighbor.

"Aren't you a dear to bring it to me, Melissa," she said.

"*Elisa,*" Elisa corrected her.

"Well, it won't be happening much longer," said Mrs. Mitchell. "My husband and I are going to be moving in a couple of months. So you won't have to worry about our mail being mixed up."

"Where are you moving to?" asked Elisa. She was glad that her family wasn't moving away.

"Connecticut. We bought a house there. Perhaps you and your parents will come and visit," Mrs. Mitchell said, smiling.

"Oh goody. I'll tell my mother what you said about visiting you," said Elisa.

Back downstairs, Elisa repeated their neighbor's invitation. "Mrs. Mitchell said we can come and visit her after she moves," she told her mother.

"Moves? Is she moving?" Mrs. Michaels sounded very surprised.

Elisa nodded. "She is moving to Connecticut."

"I didn't know that," said Mrs. Michaels. She

rushed over to the telephone and began dialing a number.

Elisa went to get her crayons. She decided she would make a picture for Russell. Then he would know she was sorry that Airmail had borrowed his Cub Scout scarf.

Elisa made three drawings while her mother talked excitedly on the phone. As soon as she hung up from one call, she made another. Elisa wondered what all the excitement was about.

That evening, when the family was eating supper, Mrs. Michaels made an announcement.

"I have a surprise for you," she told Russell and Elisa.

"Chocolate ice cream for dessert?" asked Russell eagerly.

"No," said Mrs. Michaels.

"I knew that," said Elisa. "Because I went shopping with Mommy this afternoon and I know we didn't buy any chocolate ice cream. We bought strawberries," she told Russell.

"Aw, that's not so special," said Russell.

"This surprise isn't something to eat," said Mrs. Michaels. "It's something much bigger and much better. It's a —"

"Present?" asked Russell. "What is it?" he wanted to know.

"For some time now your father and I have thought this apartment was too small for us. So we're going to move," said Mrs. Michaels.

"Move? I don't want to move," protested Russell. "I like it here. This is my home."

"I don't want to move either." Elisa began to cry. "Why can't we stay?"

"If we move, I'll miss my friends, and my Cub Scouts, and . . . everything," Russell complained.

Mr. Michaels got up from the table and began to clear the dishes away. "We are going to move . . . and not move," he said. "So you don't have to get upset about anything."

"How can we move and not move?" asked Russell. This was not a time for jokes and riddles. Moving was serious business, and he didn't like it one bit.

"We are moving to a bigger apartment in this

same building," said Mrs. Michaels. "It's on the fourth floor. We'll have more room but our address will remain the same."

"Are we moving to apartment four-H?" asked Elisa. She wiped her eyes with her napkin.

"Yes," said her mother.

"How did you know?" asked Russell. He turned to look at his sister.

"Elisa discovered that the Mitchells are moving to Connecticut. And since their apartment is much larger than this one, it is just the perfect solution," said Mr. Michaels.

"You'll still be attending the same school with your same friends," said Mrs. Michaels. "And now, Russell, you will have your own bedroom and all the privacy you want."

"So we're *not* moving," announced Russell with relief.

"We aren't and we are," said his father.

Elisa took a drink of her milk and thought about what her father had said. "We aren't and we are," she repeated, smiling. It was like a joke.

"And there's another surprise for you both too," said Mrs. Michaels.

"Another one?" gasped Russell. This was getting to be too much. "Is this one chocolate ice cream?"

"It's a baby," said Mrs. Michaels quickly. "We're going to have a baby."

"We are?" asked Elisa, amazed.

"Another one?" asked Russell. "Elisa's our baby. How come we're getting another one?"

"Elisa is not a baby any longer," said Mrs. Michaels. "She is getting bigger every day. And in the fall she will no longer be in nursery school. She'll be in kindergarten."

"I'm getting a teeny-tiny bit bigger every day," Elisa announced. "And so are you," she told Russell.

"And so is our baby," said Mr. Michaels.

"How do you know? Did you know about this surprise already?" asked Elisa.

"Yes I did," her father admitted.

"When is the baby coming?" Russell wanted to know.

"In October. After the new school year begins," said Mrs. Michaels.

"Is the baby a boy or a girl?" asked Russell.

"That will be a surprise for all of us," said Mr.

Michaels. "You may have another sister, Russell, or perhaps this time you will have a little brother."

"Let's vote," said Russell. He had been learning about elections at school. "I want a brother," he said. "What do you vote for, Dad?"

"A baby isn't something you vote for," said Mr. Michaels.

"I want a sister," said Elisa.

"We'll just have to wait until October and see," said Mrs. Michaels.

"How long is it till October?" asked Elisa.

"Count it out," said Mr. Michaels. "This is May. What comes next?"

"May, June, July, August, September, October!" shouted Elisa. She knew all the days of the week and all the months of the year. "That's awfully far away," she complained.

"It seems far away now," admitted Mrs. Michaels. "But it will be here before we know it. And we have to do a lot of things before then."

"Like what?" asked Russell suspiciously.

"Like move into our new apartment," said his father.

"And start kindergarten," added Elisa.

Mr. Michaels brought the bowl of strawberries to the table. He began to spoon them into smaller bowls for everyone.

"So. What do you think of the surprise now?" he asked his children.

Elisa stopped eating her strawberries. "It's not one surprise, it's two," she counted. "Moving to the fourth floor is a surprise, and the new baby is another surprise."

"That's right," agreed Russell.

"Here's a third surprise," said Mrs. Michaels as her husband brought a plate of cookies from the kitchen and put them on the table.

"All right. Cookies," said Russell eagerly. He reached over and grabbed one of them.

Elisa wasn't surprised by the cookies. After all, she had taken them off the shelf and put them in the shopping cart herself this very afternoon. Helping her mother with the groceries was another proof that she was getting bigger. But she kept thinking about the other two surprises.

"I like the surprises," Elisa announced. "I'm

glad we're going to have a baby."

"So am I," said Mr. Michaels. "Especially if the baby grows up to be as nice as you and Russell."

"Can I have another cookie?" asked Russell.

"Guess What?"

Now that Elisa had learned the double surprise from her parents, she wanted to share the big news with everyone she knew.

"Guess what?" she said to Nora and Teddy when she met them in front of the building the next morning.

"You lost a tooth?" guessed Nora.

40

"You found a quarter?" guessed Teddy.

"No, no, no!" shouted Elisa excitedly. "We're going to get a baby. In October. Either a boy or a girl."

"That's great," said Nora. "I wish we had a baby."

"And guess something else," said Elisa impatiently.

"I give up," said Teddy.

"We're going to move."

"Oh," moaned Teddy. "That's bad news. I don't want you to move away. I'll miss you too much."

"It's *not* bad news," said Elisa, laughing. She could hardly wait to tell her friends the other part of the surprise. "We're moving right inside this building. We're going to live on the fourth floor."

"The fourth floor!" gasped Teddy. "Then you'll live even nearer to us than ever." Nora and Teddy and their parents had an apartment on the seventh floor. "The fourth floor is closer to the seventh than the second floor is," he added.

"Isn't that a good surprise?" asked Elisa.

"It sure is," said Nora. "Soon I'll be old enough to be a baby-sitter. And I'll be able to come and take care of your baby. I'm glad you're just moving inside our building and not far away."

"Me too," said Elisa.

She saw their elderly friend Mrs. Wurmbrand walking toward them. "I've got to tell her the big news," she said, running off.

"Mrs. Wurmbrand. Guess what?" she shouted to their short, white-haired neighbor.

"You have new eyeglasses," guessed the old woman. "Just like me."

"That's old news," said Elisa. "I've had my glasses a long time already. Now I have new news." And she told Mrs. Wurmbrand about the baby and about moving.

The good thing about living in a big apartment building with lots of other people was that there were so many neighbors Elisa could share her news with.

She also told her news on the telephone. Now that she was getting bigger, sometimes she answered the phone for her parents if they were busy. That afternoon, as her mother was preparing lunch, the phone rang.

"Hello," Elisa called into the receiver.

"Elisa, honey. What are you doing?" asked her grandmother.

"I'm talking on the telephone," Elisa reported.

"So you are. And so am I," said her grandmother. "How are things?"

"Oh Grandma, guess what?" asked Elisa. She then proceeded to tell her grandmother all the news.

"In October, I am going to come for a long visit," said her grandmother. "Then I'll be able to visit with you and help your mother with the baby, too."

"Will you really sleep at our house for a long time?" asked Elisa.

"Absolutely. Positively," her grandmother promised. "And I'll bring a new outfit for Airmail."

"Oh goody, goody!" Elisa shouted into the phone. Since her grandmother had been the one to make Airmail, she would know exactly what size to make new clothing for the doll.

"And we'll all stay in the new apartment. Four-H," Elisa announced.

Before Elisa and her family could move into their new apartment, the Mitchells had to move out. Mr. and Mrs. Mitchell were planning to move at the end of July. Elisa went upstairs with her mother to discuss a few details of the move.

Mrs. Michaels wanted to measure the windows so she could begin making some curtains.

While the adults talked about boring things like windows, Elisa walked around the apartment. It was funny to think that this would soon be her home. Now it was filled with the Mitchells' furniture. Soon Elisa's bed and her toys and the little table and chairs and all of the things she knew so well would be here instead of downstairs. She wondered which bedroom would be hers and which one Russell's. Russell was especially thrilled about having his own room. Elisa did not share his enthusiasm. She liked having him in his bed across the room from her. It would be scary to be all alone.

"What color would you like your room painted?" asked Mrs. Michaels. "You can pick the color you like best."

"Any color at all?" asked Elisa.

"Sure," said her mother. "And Russell can pick the color he likes."

There were going to be a lot of new things happening when the family moved into apartment 4H. Russell was going to get a real desk all his own for doing his homework. There would be space now for a piano, too.

Soon after the Mitchells moved out, painters came and laid big canvas sheets called drop cloths all over the floor of the new apartment. Then they began work. Elisa had selected a pale-yellow color for her room. "It's just like sunshine," said Mrs. Michaels when the painters had completed their work. Elisa felt proud of her choice. Picking her own color for her own room had been a very grown up thing to do.

After the painters were gone, the children were able to walk around and around in their new apartment. None of their furniture was here yet, and their footsteps and voices echoed throughout the rooms. Elisa sat on the floor in her empty room and tried to imagine what it would be like when her bed was there. She wondered if Airmail would like this room as much as the old one downstairs on the second floor.

Elisa left her room and went looking for Russell. "This is where I'm going to put my new desk," he said, pointing to one wall of his new bedroom. "But from now on, you can't just walk in here. You have to knock on my door first," he told his sister.

"I don't care," said Elisa. She ran down the hallway of the new apartment, and Russell began chasing her through the empty rooms.

"Yahoo!" Russell called as he ran.

"Yahoo!" Elisa copied him even before he could hear the natural echo of his voice.

Russell reached out to grab his sister. Elisa squealed with pleasure. She loved playing with Russell. She ran through the living room and back into the hallway between their bedrooms and the room for the new baby. Russell was about to catch her when she ran into the bathroom. She closed the door behind her really hard, with a loud bang.

"You can't catch me," she shouted through the door to Russell.

"Yes I can!" Russell responded, and he grabbed hard on the doorknob.

Suddenly the knob came off in his hand. The knob on Elisa's side fell onto the tile floor of the bathroom. Elisa picked it up.

"You broke it!" she called to Russell. "I didn't do it. You did. You broke it."

Russell tried to insert his doorknob back into the hole in the bathroom door. But it wouldn't stay.

"You better come out," he called to Elisa.

Elisa tried to open the door. But she couldn't make her doorknob fit into the hole either. She tried pushing on the door, but it wouldn't open.

"I can't!" she shouted.

Russell tried to open the door from the outside. He couldn't do it either. He bent down and tried to peek through the hole where the doorknobs fit. It was hard to see much of anything. "Don't go away," he instructed his sister. "I'll get Mom."

Elisa sat down on the tile floor. It felt cold on her bare legs. She put the thumb of her right hand into her mouth and traced the pattern of the tiles with a finger of her left hand. She wondered how long it would take until her mother was able to open the door. She wished she had a rug to sit on and she wished Airmail was with her for company.

"Elisa," a voice called out. It was Mrs. Michaels', "I'm trying to open this door."

"I want to come out," Elisa called back.

"I know, honey, but we have to figure out how to get the door open."

"What are you doing in there?" Russell wanted to know.

"I'm sucking my thumb," said Elisa, removing her right thumb from her mouth.

"You haven't done that for a long time," Russell commented.

"Elisa," her mother called to her through the closed door. "I have to get Mr. Harvey, the super. He'll know how to help us. Russell will stay here in the apartment to keep you company. I'll be right back."

Elisa put her thumb back in her mouth and began twisting bits of her hair with her other hand. She looked around the bathroom. Her legs felt cold and she was beginning to feel a little bit hungry. It must be lunchtime by now. Maybe she was going to be locked inside the bathroom all day long. Maybe they would never be able to get her out.

Elisa wondered if she would have to live inside the bathroom forever and ever. She began to cry softly as she thought about not going to kindergarten in September. She wouldn't be able to see the new baby when it was born either.

"Elisa?"

It was Russell's voice calling to her.

"Are you crying?" he asked her.

"I'm scared," Elisa responded.

"Don't be scared," her brother said. "Stick your finger through the hole."

Elisa stood up and put a finger through the little hole where the doorknobs had been.

She felt something touching her finger. It was one of Russell's hands holding her finger.

"I'll stay here and keep you company," he said.

Elisa sniffed back some more tears. It was less scary being locked in the bathroom now that Russell was holding her finger.

"How many days is it?" she asked.

"Days? What are you talking about?" asked Russell.

"How many days have I been locked in here?"

"Days? You've been in there about ten minutes," said Russell. "And when Mr. Harvey comes, he'll get you out right away. You'll see."

Mr. Harvey came with his big case of tools. He

didn't get Elisa out right away. After he poked around unsuccessfully with the door lock, he removed the pins that held the hinges together at the top and bottom of the bathroom door. Then he pulled the door away from its frame. Suddenly the little bathroom was filled with light. Mr. Harvey and Mrs. Michaels and Russell stood in the doorway smiling. Elisa was free.

"Poor baby," soothed Mrs. Michaels.

Elisa put her arms around her mother's round body.

"Were you very scared?" asked Mrs. Michaels.

Now that the door was off, Elisa wasn't scared at all. She stopped hugging her mother and stood back. "I'm not a baby," she said. "I'm your big girl."

"Of course you are," said Mrs. Michaels. "You were very grown up taking care of yourself in the bathroom."

Mr. Harvey reattached the hinges on the bathroom door. Then he fixed the doorknobs so they wouldn't fall off again.

"You must both be starving. It's way past lunchtime," commented Mrs. Michaels to her children after the building superintendent had gone. "What do you say we celebrate Elisa's release from the bathroom by getting some pizza for lunch?"

"Yippee!" shouted Russell, and his voice echoed through the empty rooms.

"Yippee!" Elisa called out too. She ran after Russell to the front door of the apartment. Mrs. Michaels joined them, and they went out into the hallway to wait for the elevator.

"Uh-oh," said Elisa as the three of them entered the elevator.

"What is it?" asked Mrs. Michaels and Russell at the same time.

"I have to go to the bathroom," said Elisa.

The Accident

Usually when people move from one place to another, they need to hire a huge truck to transport their furniture for them. Elisa and Russell often saw such trucks on the street. Strong workers carried pieces of furniture into and out of the trucks. When the Mitchells moved, a big moving van came to cart their belongings to their new home in Connecticut.

"We won't need a truck," said Mr. Michaels. "But I'm not strong enough to carry all our furniture by myself."

"I can help," offered Russell. "Look at my muscles." He rolled up the sleeve of his shirt so his father could feel the muscle in his arm.

"Not bad," said Mr. Michaels. "You can help. But we'll need more help too."

Two men from a moving company were scheduled to come on the last day of August. They would take the furniture from the Michaelses' apartment on the second floor up to the new apartment on the fourth floor.

In preparation for the move, Mrs. Michaels began collecting empty cartons from the supermarket to use in packing. Even though they were moving up only two flights of stairs, there was a lot of work to be done before the moving men came. All the books had to be removed from the bookshelves and put in boxes. Otherwise, the movers would not be able to carry them to the new apartment.

Mr. Michaels rolled up the big living-room rug and started removing all the pictures from the walls of the apartment too.

At the same time, Mrs. Michaels was sorting through all their possessions. "You don't play with these baby toys anymore," she pointed out to Elisa as she packed some simple wooden puzzles away. "I'll save these for the baby to grow into." She also took the books with cardboard pages that Elisa used to read and put them in the box.

Elisa scowled. She didn't like to see all her old things put away for the baby. Even if she was going to begin kindergarten next month, she still liked to play with those old toys and puzzles sometimes. Why should they all go to the baby? Elisa grabbed her box of pastel chalks. The baby couldn't have those. Elisa walked into the living room. It looked strange without the pictures that usually hung there. Picking out the red chalk, which was her favorite, Elisa began to draw a picture of a house on the wall.

Mrs. Michaels gasped when she walked into the room a few minutes later. "What are you doing?" she asked, sounding displeased.

"I drew you a picture," said Elisa. She stood back to see what she had done. She knew she wasn't supposed to draw on the wall, but somehow she had just wanted to do it anyway.

"You know we don't draw on walls," scolded her mother. "Why don't you come help me with the packing."

Frowning, Elisa followed her mother into the kitchen. Usually her mother admired her pictures. Even though she knew it had been wrong to mark the wall, she felt angry, not sorry.

Mrs. Michaels removed dishes from the kitchen cabinets and began packing the dishes into cartons. She showed Elisa how to wrap each dish in newspaper so it wouldn't get broken.

"That's great," said her mother when Elisa carefully wrapped a cup in a large piece of newspaper. "You're a big help."

"I never saw that before," Elisa said, admiring a small china vase her mother was taking down from a top shelf in the kitchen cabinet.

"This was a wedding present," said Mrs. Michaels, looking at it. "It's called a bud vase, because you can only put a single flower in it." She handed the bud vase to her daughter.

Elisa stroked the little vase. It looked just the right size for her dolls to use if they had a flower. There were tiny flowers painted all over the outside of the vase. If you put a flower inside, there would be a flower inside and flowers outside at the same time, she thought. She handed it back to her mother, and Mrs. Michaels packed it away.

After a while Mrs. Michaels remembered that she had to arrange with the telephone company to have their phone calls come to the new apartment. While her mother was speaking on the phone, Elisa rummaged through the carton of wrapped dishes and looked for the little bud vase.

She removed the newspaper that was protecting it and admired the vase again. It was so small and pretty—more like a toy than something that belonged to a grown-up. She wished that it was hers. She would fill it with water and put a little flower inside for her dolls.

Elisa didn't have any flowers, but she thought she could still put some water inside the vase. She took it and went into the bathroom. In the bathroom was a small stool, which she used when she washed her hands at the sink. She pushed the stool into position and stood on it. Then she turned on the water faucet so she could fill the vase. But while she was filling it, the little bud vase slipped out of Elisa's wet hand and crashed into the basin.

One moment there had been a darling little vase and now suddenly there were just broken pieces of the china. Elisa turned off the water. For a long time she stared at the fragments of the vase. She could not believe that she had done something so terrible. It was even naughtier than drawing a picture on the wall. She knew her mother would be angry. Just thinking about what her mother would say made Elisa begin to cry.

Maybe her mother wouldn't remember the vase, she thought. It had been in the cupboard for a long, long time, and Elisa had never even seen it before. Maybe when her mother unpacked in the new apartment, she would forget all about it. Quickly Elisa picked up all the pieces of the vase. Maybe she could hide them so her mother would never find out. She took the pieces into the bedroom she shared with Russell and opened the bottom drawer in their dresser. Elisa found a sweater and wrapped

it around the pieces of the vase. Then she closed the drawer.

Mrs. Michaels came into the bedroom. "Are you all right?" she immediately asked Elisa. "You look all flushed." She put her hand to Elisa's forehead.

Feeling her mother's hand resting gently on her head, Elisa wanted to confess what had happened. But Elisa saw that her mother was smiling. If she told her about the vase, the smile would disappear.

"No. You don't seem to have a fever," said Mrs. Michaels, sounding relieved. "I guess it's just this hot summer weather. Come into the kitchen for a cold drink. I was just going to fix us a little lunch." She put her arms around Elisa and gave her a quick hug.

"I'm not hungry," said Elisa, pulling away.

"Neither am I," said her mother. "It's this heat."

She brought Elisa into the bathroom and washed her daughter's face with cool water. "I'll take you to the wading pool in the park this afternoon. That will make you feel better."

Elisa didn't feel better. She felt worse and worse. She wished she had told her mother right away about what she had done. Now, the longer she waited, the worse she felt. If only she could undo her mischief. But when she put her bathing suit on before going to the park, Elisa was struck by a wonderful idea.

On the top shelf in their bedroom were all of the models that Russell had constructed. He was very good at building them. He had made a space shuttle and several ships. One was called the *Titanic* and another was the U.S.S. *Arizona*. Maybe Russell could take the special glue he used for the models and repair the little bud vase. He had once explained to her that the glue he used was very strong.

In the late afternoon, when Russell returned from playing with Jeremy, Elisa approached him. "Could you glue something for me?" she asked her brother.

"What?" he wanted to know.

"It's a secret," said Elisa.

"How can I glue it if it's a secret?" Russell asked, puzzled.

"First tell me yes or no," Elisa insisted.

"Yes or no what?"

"Yes or no can you glue it for me," Elisa demanded.

"I guess so," said Russell, shrugging his shoulders. "All right, yes."

"Good," said Elisa, breaking into a smile.

She opened the bottom drawer of the chest and removed the sweater. Russell was curious.

"You want me to glue a sweater?" he asked.

"No, silly," said Elisa. She unwrapped the sweater and showed him the pieces of the vase. "Glue this."

"It's Mom's little vase," Russell guessed when he saw the pieces.

"I broke it," Elisa whispered.

"Does she know?" Russell whispered back, even though the two were alone in the room.

Elisa shook her head. Tears welled in her eyes. "I just wanted to put a little water in it," she told him.

"I bet I can fix it," said Russell. He went to look for his glue. Then he sat down at the little table in their room and spread out all the pieces. "Is all of it here?" he asked.

"I think so," said Elisa hopefully. She was sure she hadn't left any in the sink.

Russell looked through all the pieces until he found two that fit together. He carefully spread a bit of glue on each piece and attached them. Elisa noticed that the little flowers on the china joined and became whole, just like when she worked on a jigsaw puzzle. She began looking in the pile of fragments to help her brother match the pieces. Russell had to wait until the bits of china held fast before he could attach the next piece.

When it was suppertime, the vase was only half put together, but already Elisa was feeling better. Russell left the pieces to dry while they ate.

Elisa ate all of her hamburger and a whole ear of corn. Now that it looked as if Russell was going to succeed in repairing the vase, her appetite had returned.

After supper Russell glued the remaining pieces together. Elisa thought it was almost like magic to see the little broken pieces turning back into the pretty vase.

"Oh, Russell, you're so smart," said Elisa admiringly.

Russell nodded his head in agreement. "I did a pretty good job," he said proudly. "But it has to dry overnight." He hid the vase on the shelf behind his models.

"I smell modeling glue," remarked Mr. Michaels when he came into the bedroom before the children went to sleep.

"Yeah," said Russell.

"What are you making this time?" asked his father.

"Oh, just something," said Russell.

"It's a surprise," added Elisa.

"Oh, good," said Mr. Michaels. "I love surprises."

"Like the baby," said Elisa. "That's going to be a surprise."

"Yes, it is," agreed her father, and he gave them each a good-night kiss.

In the morning the vase was completely dry. You had to look very closely to see the tiny lines where it had been broken. Russell gave the vase to Elisa. "You better tell Mom now and get it over with," he said.

Elisa nodded her head. She went into the kitchen holding the vase.

"What are you doing with that?" asked her mother. "I thought we packed it away yesterday."

"We did. But I took it out of the box," said Elisa. "And then I broke it. It was an accident. I didn't do it on purpose." Now that she was telling, the words all seemed to rush out of her mouth.

"You broke it? It looks fine to me," said Mrs. Michaels.

"That's because Russell did such a good job fixing it," said Elisa.

Mrs. Michaels took the vase and examined it. "Russell," she called out sharply.

Elisa felt awful. It was bad enough that she had done such a terrible thing. She didn't mean to get Russell into trouble too.

Russell came into the kitchen. "Russell, this is the best job you've done yet," said his mother, admiring his handiwork. "I can't believe how well you matched up these pieces. That takes great skill."

Russell beamed. "It wasn't so hard," he said.

"Elisa helped me match up the pieces."

"I'm especially proud of you for helping Elisa. I like it when the two of you cooperate and help each other."

Elisa smiled with relief. Her mother wasn't angry at them after all.

"If Russell's violin broke," Mrs. Michaels said, "he might be able to glue it together, but the music wouldn't sound the same afterward. And the same with this vase. It almost looks like new, Elisa, but perhaps it won't be able to hold water without leaking. You must think twice about touching things and remember to be more careful in the future." Mrs. Michaels paused for a moment, thinking. "Especially with the new baby. I handled you very carefully when you were newborn babies. And you're going to need to do the same with your little sister or brother."

"I will," said Russell.

"I will too," said Elisa. "I'll be careful. I promise." She gave her mother a hug, which wasn't easy these days, as her mother had grown so big with the new baby inside her.

"I know you will," said Mrs. Michaels. "Our baby is going to be very lucky to have such a nice big brother and sister as both of you."

Welcome Home

On a Friday morning in early October, Elisa woke in her old bed in her new room. Her door was open and it was quiet in the apartment. She guessed she was the first one to wake up this morning. Instead of getting out of bed, she snuggled under her cover and looked around in the dim light. During her first few nights here, she had had trouble falling asleep. But now she was getting more used to being alone in the dark. And she discovered that she liked her new room after all.

Elisa felt a lump under her shoulder and reached to retrieve it. The lump was Airmail. She was wearing the new flannel nightgown that Grandma had made for her. Seeing it reminded Elisa that her grandmother was staying with them. Elisa got out of bed and went to see if her grandmother was awake yet.

Elisa found her grandmother in the kitchen. She had big news. In the middle of the night, while Elisa and Russell were sleeping, their mother had gone off to the hospital. Neither of the children had heard her leave with their father.

"You have a new baby brother!" Grandma announced. "He was born at dawn."

"Are you sure?" asked Elisa. She had so hoped the new baby would be a sister.

"Absolutely. Positively," said the older woman. "His name is Marshall."

"Marshall?" said Russell, who had just then

appeared in the kitchen doorway. He thought it over and nodded approvingly. "I'm glad it's a boy," he said.

"Marshall," said Elisa. "Marshall." She tried the name a few times to get used to it. "Marshall. It sounds a little like marshmallow. I like marshmallows."

"And you'll like this baby, too," said their grandmother.

Even though they didn't get a new baby brother every day of the week, the children still had to go off to school.

"Did Daddy go to work?" asked Elisa when they were dressed and eating breakfast.

"No, he's at the hospital visiting with your mother. He was up all night, so he'll be coming home soon to get some sleep."

"In the middle of the day?" asked Elisa, surprised.

"Well, just a bit of a nap, I suppose," said their grandmother. "This evening he's going to take all of us to the hospital to see Marshall and your mother."

"Oh, goody!" said Elisa. She missed her mother and was glad she'd get to see her. "How long till Mommy comes home?" she wanted to know.

"She's coming home on Sunday morning," said their grandmother. "You can make a sign to welcome her when you come home from school."

Now that she was in kindergarten, Elisa went to the same school building as Russell. He was in fourth grade. Elisa wondered if fourth grade was as much fun as kindergarten. She loved her teacher. Ms. Cassedy had been Russell's teacher a long time ago, when he was in kindergarten.

At school, it didn't take long until everyone in Elisa's class had heard the big news about her new baby brother. In fact, Ms. Cassedy took a count among the students. There were seventeen children in Elisa's class, and eight of them had babies at home. Five babies were girls, and counting Marshall, three babies were boys. Two of the baby girls were named Jessica, and there was a Jessica in Elisa's kindergarten class, too.

The class talked about mommies going to hospitals when babies were born. "Last summer Russell and I went to the hospital so we could see what it looks like," Elisa told her teacher.

Ms. Cassedy picked Elisa to be the helper during juice-and-cookie time. "I know you will be a big help to your mother, too," said Ms. Cassedy as she watched Elisa put a chocolate-chip cookie on a napkin at each place on the tables.

There were also cookies waiting for Elisa and Russell when they got home from school. "Can I make my sign now?" asked Elisa after she finished her cookies and her glass of milk.

"I want to make a sign too," said Russell when he heard what Elisa was going to do.

"Let's make a big, big one together," said Elisa. "We could hang it outside in the hallway as a surprise."

"We made a banner at school once," Russell remembered. "We used an old sheet." He turned to his grandmother. "Could we have a sheet to use?" he asked.

"I'll see what I can find," she said.

"Maybe Mommy won't want us to color on a sheet," said Elisa when their grandmother presented the children with a large white bed sheet to use.

"This is a very special occasion," said their grandmother. "So it's all right to paint on a sheet this time."

Russell and Elisa spread out the sheet on the floor. Russell made huge block letters and Elisa helped to fill them in. The banner said:

WELCOME HOME MOMMY

They used every color in Russell's paint set and all of Elisa's crayons. Elisa tried using her pastel chalks, too, but they smudged on the sheet. Russell drew cars and trucks and people. Elisa made flowers all around the banner.

"We'll ask Henry to let us put this up in the lobby," Russell decided. Henry was the doorman of their building. He stood at the entrance of the building and greeted everyone entering or leaving.

"In the lobby?" asked Elisa jumping up with delight.

"Sure. Then everyone in the whole building can see it," said Russell.

It seemed like a great idea.

In the evening, after an early supper, they all

went to the hospital. "You're lucky that this hospital has a new rule permitting children to visit their parents," said Grandma.

They stopped at the florist and bought a big bouquet of flowers. And they stopped at the ice-cream store and bought some butter-pecan ice cream. It was their mother's favorite flavor. Even though they had visited the hospital during the summer and seen the room where the babies stayed, it was extra exciting to go now. This time they were going to see their own baby.

"Which one is Marshall?" asked Elisa as they looked through the window of the nursery.

"He's that big one on the end," said her father proudly.

Russell and Elisa stared at their new brother. The truth was he didn't look so very different from most of the other babies.

"Why is he wearing a hat inside the hospital?" asked Elisa.

All the babies had little caps on their heads.

"To keep his head warm, silly," said Russell.

"My head is warm without a hat," she said.

"That's because you have hair."

"Doesn't Marshall have any hair?" Elisa asked.

"Very little," said their father.

"You were bald for a long time when you were a baby," their grandmother said, remembering.

"I was?" Elisa rubbed her head in amazement. She had seen her baby pictures, but she couldn't really believe that she had once been bald.

Next they went into the room to visit their mother. She was sitting up in the hospital bed, and she looked just like always, except her stomach was much flatter than it had been the day before.

"How do you like your baby brother?" she asked as she gave Elisa and Russell each a big hug.

"He's okay," said Russell. "I'm glad he's a boy."

"He's wearing a hat to keep his head warm because he doesn't have any hair," Elisa told her mother.

Their grandmother put the flowers they had brought into a glass vase, which one of the nurses gave her. Mr. Michaels handed his wife the bag with the ice cream. "We brought you a little treat," he said.

Mrs. Michaels opened the bag, and then she removed the plastic lid from the container. "My favorite flavor," she said, smiling. "Do you want a taste?" she asked the children.

Though both Russell and Elisa loved ice cream, neither of them liked it with nuts inside. So they both said no. "Good," laughed their mother. "There's more for me."

"We're going to stop and buy ourselves some chocolate ice cream on the way home," said Mr. Michaels.

Russell and Elisa broke into grins. That was a surprise they hadn't expected.

All day Saturday they were busy getting ready for Mrs. Michaels's return home. Their grandmother put a clean sheet on the crib for the baby. Mr. Michaels went out and bought more flowers for the apartment. Elisa started making more signs. Soon there were signs in the bathroom, the kitchen, her parents' bedroom, and the living room, too. They all said WELCOME HOME MOMMY.

In the late afternoon Mr. Michaels went down to the lobby of their building with Russell and Elisa

and the banner and some thumbtacks. Mr. Harvey lent Mr. Michaels a ladder, and he was able to put up the banner.

It looked wonderful hanging on the wall. Russell and Elisa were very proud of their handiwork. They knew their mother would be very surprised to see such a giant banner waiting to greet her when she arrived home the next morning.

Henry the doorman agreed. He looked up at their banner and admired it. "Your mother will just love that," he said, smiling at the children.

On Sunday morning Elisa woke in her new bedroom extra early. She was very excited that her mother was coming home today. She was also excited that her baby brother would be coming home too. Elisa got out of bed and put on her furry bedroom slippers. She wanted to peek in Marshall's room and imagine what it would look like when he was in it.

When Marshall grew up, he would think they had always lived in apartment 4H. He wouldn't know what it was like to have lived in their smaller apartment on the second floor, she thought. He would see her wearing her glasses and he would think she had always worn them. Maybe when he got older, he would need to wear glasses too.

She wondered how long it would be before she could play real games with him, the way she played with Russell. She would teach him all the ABC's, just the way Russell had taught them to her.

As soon as he had eaten breakfast, Mr. Michaels left for the hospital. Before long he would be back with Mrs. Michaels and Marshall in a taxi. Elisa could hardly wait.

Suddenly she was struck by a terrible thought.

"Grandma," she said. "All our signs say 'Welcome home, Mommy.' None of them say 'Marshall.'"

"It doesn't matter," said Russell. "Marshall can't read. He won't know what the signs say."

"I don't care," said Elisa. "We should have a sign to welcome *him* home too."

"There isn't much time," said their grandmother. "You used up all the paper in the house yesterday. And I don't have another bed sheet to spare, either."

"I know what!" shouted Elisa. "I don't need paper or a sheet."

She ran to her room and got her box of pastels. She hadn't really used them since the day her mother had scolded her for drawing on the wall in their old apartment. "Mommy only lets me draw with these in the park, because she says it looks messy in front of the house. But this is special. Can't I make a sign right now on the sidewalk outside? Just this once?"

"You better check with Henry or Mr. Harvey first," suggested her grandmother.

"Sure," said Henry when Elisa asked him. "I know Mr. Harvey won't mind this one time. We can't have people writing on the sidewalk every day. But this is a special big day."

Elisa got down on her hands and knees in front of the building and set to work. You better hurry," said Russell. "Let me help you." He spelled out the name of their new brother for Elisa. Then he made big block letters the way he had done for the banner. Elisa worked hard coloring them in with her red and yellow and green pastels. She was just fin-

80

ishing her task when the taxi pulled up in front of the house.

Elisa stood up and wiped her hands on her jeans. She looked at the taxi and saw her mother and father sitting close together in the backseat. But where was Marshall? For a moment Elisa felt worried. Could her parents have forgotten him at the hospital? Then the taxi door opened and she saw that her mother was holding a bundle of blankets. She could see Marshall's little cap.

Elisa looked down at her message on the sidewalk. It was big and clear. It didn't really matter that the new baby couldn't read. She wanted everyone in the whole building and everyone on their whole street to be able to see what she had written:

WELCOME HOME MARSHALL

She stood proudly watching as her father got out first and began helping her mother out of the taxi. Suddenly, just as her mother was about to emerge from the car, an exciting thought occurred to Elisa.

"Grandma," she called with delight. "Guess what?

Even though I'm always going to be Russell's little sister, now I'm a big sister too. I'm Marshall's big sister!"

Elisa's grandmother smiled at her and nodded. "Absolutely. Positively," she said.

COMMUNITY LIBRARY